The Golden Sandal

A MIDDLE EASTERN CINDERELLA STORY

BY REBECCA HICKOX

ILLUSTRATED BY WILL HILLENBRAND

HOLIDAY HOUSE/NEW YORK

The author and illustrator would like to thank Dr. Jean-Marc Ron Oppenheim
of the Middle East Institute at Columbia University for his assistance.

Text copyright © 1998 by Rebecca A. Hickox
Illustrations copyright © 1998 by Will Hillenbrand
Printed and Bound in April 2011 at
Kwong Fat Offset Printing Co., Ltd., Dongguan City, China.
7 9 11 10 8
Library of Congress Cataloging-in-Publication Data
Hickox, Rebecca A.
The golden sandal/ by Rebecca A. Hickox;
illustrated by Will Hillenbrand. – 1st ed.
p.   cm. / Based on a Cinderella story from Iraq called
"The little red fish and the clog of gold" in Inea Bushnaq's Arab folktales.
Summary: An Iraqi version of the Cinderella story in which a kind
and beautiful girl who is mistreated by her stepmother and stepsister finds a
husband with the help of a magic fish.
ISBN 0-8234-1331-4 (reinforced)
[1. Fairy tales. 2. Folklore—Iraq.] I. Hillenbrand, Will, ill.
II. Cinderella. English. III. Title.
PZ8.H5Go 1998
[398..2' 09567' 02]–dc21
97-5071
CIP
AC
ISBN 0-8234-1513-9 (pbk.)

ISBN-13: 978-0-8234-1331-7 (hardcover)
ISBN-13: 978-0-8234-1513-7 (paperback)

for Diane
"The best elixir is a friend."
WILLIAM SOMERVILLE

RH

for Carol & Armin
WH

There once lived a fisherman whose wife had drowned, leaving him with a small daughter named Maha. Nearby lived a widow with her own young daughter. Every day she went to the fisherman's house to care for Maha, and every day she said, "You poor motherless child! I love you like my own."

"Father," begged the girl, "You should marry our good neighbor so you won't have to cook your own food or mend your own clothes, and then I can have a mother and a sister."

Her father stroked her hair. "Ah little one, I shall never marry, for stepmothers are too often jealous of another's child."

But Maha continued to beg, and by and by the fisherman and the neighbor were married.

At first all went well, but as time passed the woman saw how much the fisherman loved his daughter. She saw how lovely and clever the girl was, and how pale and clumsy her own daughter seemed in comparison. As the months went by, Maha was forced to do more and more of the work, and during the day when the fisherman was gone, her stepmother fed her nothing but a few dried dates.

One day, as Maha was walking home with a basket of three catfish which she'd been sent to fetch from her father's boat, she heard a voice.

"Luckless child! Have pity on another unfortunate. Spare my life."

The frightened girl set the basket down and found a little red fish under the others. Full of wonder, she carried the fish back to the river. As she released it, the fish spoke again.

"Allah says a kindness never goes unrewarded. Call for me any time and ask what you will."

When her father returned home, he asked what had happened to the red fish.

"What!" the stepmother scolded Maha. "You didn't tell me there was another fish. You shall have to go look for it. If you return without it, you'll be sorry."

Maha made her way, hungry and frightened, through the darkness to the river.

"Little fish," she called, "please help me. I don't know what to do."

The fish appeared at the water's edge.

"What is the trouble, my child?"

"Stepmother is angry that I brought only three fish home. If I go back empty-handed she will beat me."

"Here," replied the fish, "you will find a golden coin in my mouth. Give it to her and say you sold the fish."

The stepmother was pleased with the coin, but she loved her stepdaughter no better.

The years went by, and both girls grew into young women.

Maha worked from sunup to sunset, but each day increased her beauty inside and out. Her stepsister, on the other hand, grew selfish and mean, and many a time added to Maha's woes. When things were too hard, the poor girl would go to the river and call for the fish who always helped her in one way or another.

One day, the daughter of the master merchant was to be married. All the women of the town gathered before the wedding to sing and celebrate and watch the bride's arms and feet be painted with red henna stain. This was a time of great excitement among the unmarried girls, for it was at the women's celebration that they were seen by the mothers of young men. Whom would they choose to be brides for their sons?

The stepmother scrubbed her daughter and dressed her in their finest. Maha was left at home to carry the heavy water jugs and sweep the floor.

As soon as the others were gone, Maha ran to the river.

"Little fish, please tell me what to do. Will I be a slave to my stepmother forever?"
The fish appeared at the river's edge.
"What is it you wish, my child?"
"I wish to join the other girls at the bride's henna. I long to sing and laugh and see all the fine clothes and jewelry."

"You shall go," replied the fish, "but you won't sit near the door with the other fishermen's daughters. You shall sit on the cushions in the middle of the hall near the bride herself! Just be sure to leave the celebration before your stepmother."

On the grass of the river bank there appeared a silken gown, a pearl comb, and a pair of golden sandals. Maha washed herself, dressed in the gown and sandals, and tucked the comb into her hair.

When she entered the merchant's house, the women made a place for her next to the bride. They did not know who she was, but they could see she must be from an important family. Her stepmother and stepsister whispered to each other that she looked very much like Maha, then giggled to think of her with such fine clothes.

Maha had such a good time that she forgot to keep a close watch on her stepmother. When the woman stood up to leave, Maha rushed out another door and ran for home, but as she hurried over a footbridge, she tripped, and one of her golden sandals dropped into the water below.

She picked herself up and ran on. When her stepmother and stepsister arrived, Maha, dressed once again in rags, was sweeping the doorstep.

Several days after the wedding festivities, Tariq, the brother of the bride, went riding. He dismounted and led his horse to the river bank for a drink, but each time the horse lowered his head to drink, he shied away and refused to touch the water.

"What's the matter?" asked the young man.

He bent down and saw something glittering in the morning sun. Reaching in, he pulled out a golden sandal. There was something so delicate, so beautiful about the little shoe that he longed to meet its owner.

That evening he only ate a few bites of his meal.

"What is troubling you, my son?" asked his mother.

Tariq pulled the sandal from his robe.

"As you often say, it is time for me to marry, and I wish to marry the owner of this sandal. But who is she?"

His mother was pleased.

"Don't worry my son. I will find her."

The next day she went from house to house in the wealthy section of town, for surely the owner of such a sandal would live there. Perhaps it would even be the fine girl who came to her daughter's henna. She tried the sandal on each unmarried woman, but it fit none.

The next day she visited other parts of the city with the same luck. On the third day she came to the fishermen's huts. When Maha's stepmother saw the merchant's wife approaching, she shoved Maha into the bread oven in the yard and covered the opening with a large rock.

Despite all efforts, however, her own daughter's foot would not fit into the little sandal. Tariq's mother was about to leave when the rooster flew to the top of the oven and began crowing with all his might.

Ki-ki-ki-ko, ki-ki-ki-ko,
The one you seek is hidden below.

Tariq's mother ordered her servant to open the oven. Maha crawled out, and her foot slipped easily into the sandal. When the merchant's wife saw the beauty and kindness in the girl's eyes, she knew she'd found a worthy bride for her son.

"Here," she said, handing a purse of gold to the stepmother. "Your stepdaughter is now betrothed to my eldest son. The wedding procession shall come for her in two days time."

Even now the stepmother could not rejoice in her family's good fortune. She went to the perfumer with some of the gold and asked him to make an oil which would smell as foul as rotting fish and cause hair to fall from the head. The night before the wedding she held her breath and combed the foul potion through Maha's lovely dark hair.

The next day, the procession came and carried the bride on a litter through the streets amid much singing and dancing. Tariq waited impatiently to sign the wedding contract so he could see his bride. When he at last lifted her veil, the scent of roses filled the room and her hair was so beautiful he could not stop stroking it.

When Tariq's brother saw his happiness, he went to his mother and asked for Maha's sister. Once again the stepmother was given a bag of gold and told to prepare for a wedding.

The woman had heard of the oil's effects on Maha, so the night before the wedding she combed the reeking mixture through her own daughter's hair. The next day the procession carried the girl through the streets, but this time when the groom lifted the veil, he choked at the smell and saw that his bride's head was covered with blisters instead of hair. The girl was taken back to her mother in disgrace.

As for Maha and Tariq, they were blessed with seven children and lived their days in great joy and good fortune.

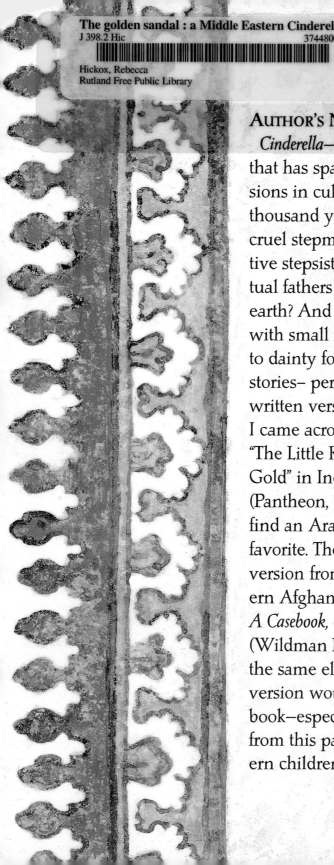

AUTHOR'S NOTE

Cinderella—what is it about this story that has spawned hundreds of versions in cultures worldwide for over a thousand years? Are there that many cruel stepmothers, lazy and unattractive stepsisters, and loving but ineffectual fathers in every corner of the earth? And what about this obsession with small feet? The suitor's attraction to dainty footwear appears in many stories– perhaps because the earliest written version is from China. When I came across a story from Iraq called "The Little Red Fish and the Clog of Gold" in Inea Bushnaq's *Arab Folktales* (Pantheon, 1986), I was delighted to find an Arabic version of this old favorite. There is another interesting version from eastern Iran and western Afghanistan recorded in *Cinderella: A Casebook,* edited by Alan Dundes, (Wildman Press, 1983) with many of the same elements. I thought the Iraqi version would make a good picture book—especially since the only tales from this part of the world most western children know are from the *Arabian Nights.* I used the storyteller's prerogative to shorten and simplify the story a bit, but with so many versions in the world already, I doubt the ultimate rags-to-riches girl will mind one more slight variation.

ILLUSTRATOR'S NOTE

The artwork for this book was done on vellum—a translucent paper. For each picture, a copy of the final pencil drawing was placed in reverse on the underside of the vellum. Some underpainting was then done with oil paint or pastel to give the picture a color field. The picture was then drymounted with a wax tissue to a flexible bristol board to make the vellum more rigid. Finally, the picture was painted with a mixture of media including oils, oil pastel, egg tempera, watercolor, water soluble artist crayons, and a combination of 2b, 6b and 9b woodless pencils.

Much of my source material came from a book edited by Bernard Lewis, *The World of ISLAM: Faith, People , Culture* (Thames and Hudson, 1976).